Short Cuts

Mick Evans

Published by Leaf by Leaf
an imprint of Cinnamon Press
www.cinnamonpress.com

The right of Mick Evans to be identified as author of this work has been asserted by him in accordance with the Copyright, Designs and Patent Act, 1988. © 2022, Mick Evans.
ISBN 978-1-78864-939-1

British Library Cataloguing in Publication Data. A CIP record for this book can be obtained from the British Library.

Designed and typeset in Adobe Caslon Pro by Cinnamon Press.
Cover design by Adam Craig © Adam Craig.
Cinnamon Press is represented by Inpress

Acknowledgements

I wish to thank Jan Fortune for her constant support, patience, and encouragement; for believing in these pieces, and bringing them to order; for her advice and suggestions, so deft and always apposite, with the lightest of touches. Thanks are due to Adam for another wonderful cover. I thank everyone at Cinnamon Press for the remarkable work they do in nurturing and supporting writers. And I thank all those who have kept faith in me and supported my writing: Jane Belli of Ffynon Wen Writers, Dominic and Mel of write4word, who provide such a supportive forum for spoken word performance; the Dinefwr Poetry group; and, of course, Sian, for the greatest of all gifts.

Contents

To my family, for the healings

Short Cuts

Introduction

I had long harboured the desire to write prose poetry. This is not that. Rather, these pieces began as attempts at the genre and were abandoned as inappropriate to the collection on which I laboured. Cuts, in the film maker's sense then. But they would not lie down, and demanded a life and development of their own; more prose than prosody, troublesome children crying for attention; or, not to mix metaphors, fractious horses. I gave in, and let them have their head. But, still unsatisfied, more was demanded, in the form of an identity, at least a name. Clearly this overarching presence is not the poet so influential on the 20th century; rather it is a surfacing of ideas, events, and situations, from whatever place the surreal lurks.

No more is the character who turns up in Florence, with a rucksack of useful and interesting items, the Cassandra of myth, cursed to utter true prophecies but never to be believed. But pity the sufferings of all lovers with a too long deferred consummation.

These are Cuts too in the sense that they often address painful, embarrassing, or uncomfortable events or memories. And shortcuts when sometimes finding oneself 'in a dark wood' plunged into the past, disorientated, unsure how one came to be there. Or just to be, as in Blood Lines.

Some pieces are a ram-raid on experience; as in response to the overwhelming power of ballet, a welter of emotion, at the labour, pain, and discipline demanded by this art form. La Bayadere is the ballet in question. Lovers of the medium will recognise the iconic entry of the corps de ballet.

The dramatic monologue is a genre that has long fascinated me. It has a long history, with a special brand of self-revelation. I hope these pieces speak for themselves, uncovering each character's secrets and passions. And I hope the savage irony of the ending of Theatre Functionary finds its true target, having once performed the piece, and heard a cry of misguided affirmation from a member of the audience. Since then, I have not dared to repeat the experience of venting this voice from a post-Brexit wasteland.

These *Short Cuts* are then a miscellany shaped by a consciousness: some humorous, some sinister, perhaps painful, occasionally joyful shots in the dark. Hopefully, a little, but not too much, like life.

Prologue

Marlowe was stabbed with a dagger and died swearing. According to the inquest, the fatal blow, delivered through or just above the right eye socket, 'of the depth of two inches and of the width of one inch', was the result of a disagreement over Le recknynge at widow Eleanor Bull's house. The nature of this establishment is not made clear, only that there was a garden and an upper room in which the protagonists spent part of the afternoon, and some expenses accrued. Researchers of the Christopher Marlowe Society offer an alternative to the traditional interpretation of the tavern brawl, citing Marlowe's possible involvement as an agent of Walsingham, and the motive of his three companions that day who may have had cause to wish him dead.

Modern physicians describe the likely effect of the stab wound, gleaning details from the account and autopsy made at the time. Death was most likely to have been caused by 'intercranial pressure after a wound to the internal carotid artery'…Given this, one can forgive the cursing.

The dagger in question, value XIId, was of a type typically positioned at the back, slung sideways, to be readily grasped, and, if a sword was also worn, used principally as a parrying weapon, until its final function in delivering a *coup de grâce*. The width of the entry wound, one inch, suggests this was neither a stiletto nor a misericorde, long, thin weapons developed in medieval times for piercing between plates of armour. Not Hamlet's bare bodkin then.

The last word on daggers must be those of Webster, master of the short phrase, in The Duchess of Malfi, as Bosola delivers the death blow to the Cardinal:

'I do glory
That thou, which stood'st like a huge Piramid
Begun upon a large, and ample base,
Shalt end in a little point, a kind of nothing.'

Marlowe's death, be it premeditated political assassination or murder in a tavern brawl, seems more messy, ragged, brutal than our vision of, say, Tybalt and Mercutio's stage fight, iconically fought out over ten minutes in Zeffirelli's film. Tamburlaine, Faustus, and the Maltese Jew, bled out in Deptford, and other forces were at work. The complexities of characterisation, and his mighty line, would be refined by a greater genius where those elements of swordplay—cut and thrust, parrying, evasion, mischance—would find a metaphorical and linguistic as well as literal application in the drama. Marlowe's was a life and genius cut short. Already transforming the subject and scope of the stage, his was a painful reckoning.

An awakening

A night of white flesh. Dreaming body. Wake from drenched tangle. Get out. Walk, clear the mind. Up to the open spaces, where larks sing. Short grass. Pure air fresh and full of song. Famous for it. Examine. All embodiments exact. Proceed. Conversant with tree and hedgerow. Then crossing the broad savannah come upon a lane. A deep thrust into the future, green hills bosoming heavenward. The town behind me. The nipple of the bronze age barrow ahead. All that done with. Then a car. Halting. Reversing. Woman driver. In the driving seat, so to speak. Enquiring, do I want a lift. Skirt. Knees! Christ, yes! But no. Lack courage. What did that mean. Why does someone who does not know from Adam give enough of a damn to coast up and window down to suggest something. And dull enough to refuse, I being young. Perhaps there would be coffee at her kitchen table, conversation, life histories, a touch of hands as we reach for sugar. Laughter. A glance towards the stairs. Wake up. Her hands on the wheel, reach across, hand on her knee. Between her thighs. Slamming on the brakes. What the hell. Get out. Seeing you in broken shoes and drizzle. Take pity. This how you. Wake up. Coffee in her kitchen. Hands touch as we both reach for sugar. Clasping her hand. Snatch. What are you playing. Not like the other. Emptying the flat, loading the van, table, chair, boxes of books, she comes and introduces herself with enticing phrase please don't call the police can you would you take me (home). I can't, can't you see is this really necessary can't get rid she too half cut and liable to become a liability or aggressive she sits on the kerb. Twitch of neighbourly curtain. I acquiesce. Her skirt too long and she in years. Manage to follow garbled instructions to her round the houses house a quarter of a league away. And get her near enough but not in. Out the passenger door. Drive away. Inhabiting as we do a universe of missed opportunities inhibited by misread intentions. Withering, I lay a feeble claim to innocence.

The Cossack.

When the singing was over, we were introduced by a mutual friend, the bourgeois Mayor of a small provincial town in Russia, fresh from his appearance in *The Government Inspector*, in which I played the Judge. She had expressed an interest in getting to know me. Our introduction was brief, and involved tongues. She wore a fur hat, purple trousers tucked into high red boots, and a velvet cape. We walked to the station through snow. There was moonlight. I thought of troikas and how much like a Cossack she looked.

She did not wear a fur hat, nor was she ever in possession of high boots. I was learning Russian at the time, reading Lermontov's *A Hero of our Time*. No-one since Oscar Wilde has worn a cape seriously. It was high summer. She wore a thin blouse and no bra.

After we managed to stop having sex and looked at each other, we thought we had better do something, so we bought tickets for the Cambridge Folk Festival. She said she did not want it to be a dirty weekend. We took a single sleeping bag, the close confines of which proved the perfect contraceptive. It was nominally a folk festival, but at least half the acts were country and western. It rained and we took refuge in a marquee. We were kept awake all night by people singing dreary songs. The site was flanked by gardens, and a lady offered to air our sleeping bag. She returned it late in the afternoon, dry and carefully folded. Since then I have never attended a musical event that does not provide chairs or a roof.

She was a year younger than me, so when I went to college she had to make do with letters. Mine were repetitive and dull. Solace was taken in a former lover, more muscular, more handsome, with independent means, and motorised transport. The fates are mercenary. We met twice more, once in Reading, when she had asked to borrow my copies of Virginia Woolf for her university course. The last time was when she returned them. We discussed *To the Lighthouse*; a promise fulfilled, and a work of art completed. They are the red and white Hogarth Press editions, standing out a little blood-like on the shelves. Sometimes I take Virginia down and hold them, being the last things we both touched.

We were invited to a relative's wedding. When his wife divorced him and moved in with someone else, he took an eight inch kitchen knife and slashed the tyres of all the cars in her street. This proved expensive, and must have been hard work. I do not know whether the blade was straight edged or serrated. Sometimes I wonder which would have made it easier.

Another relative's best friend committed suicide after his wife left him for someone else. His friends took against her, complaining she never shed a tear for him. Why would anyone waste tears on someone they no longer loved, and were glad to be rid of?

The Cossacks were highly admired for their equestrian skills. Many were hired as cavalry by Russian and Ukrainian warlords. Their origins are mysterious. They have always had to fight for recognition and independence. Fearless warriors, they make dangerous enemies. When I took up fencing, the sabre was my weapon of choice. The 'cavalry of the Steppes' used the shashka, long associated with this noble people. It features the distinctive blade geometry of the sabre, and the strong distal taper provides a balance ideal for its slashing role. These are my terms.

The Celts

The cattle raid of Cooley

Having once trespassed on their territories, we find the faie implacable. From the borderlands in the cool evening I crept to your door. Of the green-eyes and flaxen hair and the friendly thighs. You were not unwilling. Again I make you my ritual. A libation of the strong spirit. Dark and burning in the glass. Your hair a spell that could not be broken. Your father Irish, your mother, of the fair neck, a nurse. When I injured myself in the joinery works, after the healing, she offered to remove the last stitches. Little silver scissors, and a single tug of the dark thread through the black scab. Blood came, but only very little, and I thought of our first time. You looked on, impassive. At this time I was not strong enough to fight. You helped bear my luggage, and we returned late, all trains cancelled. On your holiday trek in Africa, you slept with the guide, beneath the van; the wild beasts, the bull oxen, moving around you heavily in the night, snuffing at thin grass under unfamiliar stars. Waking at dawn, flights of birds rising through mist. It would have been better if you had never spoken of this, for afterwards you regretted our separation. Trying to heal the wound was futile. Late into the night I could see light in your bedroom. I think of you before the mirror, two of you, one a perfect image burnished by the light, both brushing long hair. Your fair skin and hair are ghostly. You loved to dance. There are ancient feuds, but now I am old I lack strength to heal them.

Blood Lines

I do not keep a diary but today, having received my DNA analysis, it seems to warrant an entry in an otherwise non-existent journal.

I have always liked to think of myself as Anglo-Saxon: I have admired the jewellery in the British Museum, and harboured a fond idea that my ancestors may have conducted guerrilla warfare against the bastard Normans. However, today has been something of a dampener. There are all kinds of caveats of course: for a start, this can only be fifty percent of the story. It would require the participation of siblings or other tribal members to get a fuller picture. This has proved something of a disappointment for my wife, too, who has also had her results, Ever since hearing from a cousin of a whiff of Italian illegitimacy in the family, she had been devoted to the idea of importing a degree of disrespectability into an otherwise conservative Baptist ancestry. Nothing doing. She is almost pure Celt, though her sisters may throw up something, if they can ever be persuaded to spit into a test tube.

I, however, find that I have, in increasing degrees, the associations of an active mongrel; with London, the Potteries, Ireland, Scotland, and, predominantly, Scandinavia. I had always known, on my maternal side, of established families from Hull and Norfolk; a North Sea connection that says something, but proves nothing, though, if we are talking Vikings, the connection with Ireland is plausible enough.

So where does this leave me? Certainly on the wrong side of the Danelaw in the Anglo Saxon Chronicle. And how far back do we go? Am I a distant echo of the *mycel hæþen here* wintering out, or of an off duty Norwegian stoker disembarking from a coaster to visit the backstreets of Glasgow, and fill the hours of a pleasant afternoon in exciting company? Or perhaps having made previous landfall, the warmth of a hearth beckons; or he sets off to a certain address, with a ring in his pocket and a hopeful offer in his heart. In all events, my Anglo Saxon dream is over. We all have to abide with a past, or by it, invented or otherwise. So now I compose myself to the possibility that in the wintry nights I tasted the tang of salt and felt the shiver of the oar in my hands. And heard in the grey dawns the keel ground on shingle. Then cries.

The Chinese

For two years I shared a flat with a girl above a Chinese takeaway. Her main aim was to prevent a meeting between myself and her mother, who had a habit of appearing unannounced. It was on the third floor, with only one access. Initially I was her foundling. Then a complication, finally a nuisance. We had a common interest in folk music. She was musical to a degree. More so than me. I purchased a second hand flute as a farewell gift, which required serious repair, as it turned out, so more a *memento mori* than plain memento—and departed for Hull, to commence teacher training, and allow her to develop a blossoming relationship with a guitarist, a serious musician. I encountered her mother only once, entering the hallway as I made a mistimed exit. As teaching was regarded as neither respectable nor remunerative, I was never acknowledged, and never forgiven. There were limited facilities but we were happy on the third floor. I danced with her once, before the relationship foundered.

She owned a blue silk dressing gown with a Chinese design of birds with long tail feathers and elongated wings, green and red. Around her breasts, thighs, and buttocks, these creatures flew as she moved. All attempts to explore their nesting grounds were firmly rebuffed. I don't know what birds they were—cranes, jays, birds of paradise, I can't be bothered. But we may as well say the transformed ones in the Willow Pattern – a design as authentically Chinese as the meals served below us. There they go, over the bridge, up and away, diverging into the porcelain sky. The fleeing lovers.

A Bird's Eye View

From. To. And alight; one by the statue of Hull's aviator, white with pigeon shit. The eternal upward gaze of the former, the corollary of flight the latter. On a bench a woman tells me how her husband beats her. At a bus stop an elderly lady, concerned for my welfare, donates biscuits from her shopping. I live in digs, a room in a council house, a late arrangement by the university, with a woman who, unsolicited, darns my socks., I feel this is an intrusion. Her daughter is a devotee of Northern Soul. Even though this is the period when the fishing fleet is being run down, there hangs over the whole area the smell of fish, from the processing factory that provides most of the employment. Avoiding contact with people, I choose not to use public transport, and walk five miles each way from my accommodation, into lectures on Eysenck and data manipulation. I watch buses pass, Gypsyville in bold white lettering on the destination boards.

One evening I pass a house with its curtains open. There is a bare, brightly-lit room where a folk band is rehearsing. They are depressingly good. I visit the Blue Bell folk club, frequented by the Carthys. I do not see them, but attend a gig at the university where Martin performs. I break one of my own rules when I have to sit on the floor. I find fame when, at the interval, he asks me to direct him to the toilet.

Later, I move into a guest room on campus, the Brynmor Jones library tower looking down on us, where a bald bespectacled figure gazes out from its High

Windows. He is rarely seen. Everyone has already formed friendships. I can't be bothered.

One of the things no-one tells you about alienation is how terrifying it is. It could be endless.

I receive an invitation to visit a great aunt in a nearby care home. After some weeks I receive a second more insistent note. I visit once, and also meet her middle-aged son. These people cannot help me, and I do not call again. In my letters home I have nothing to tell them.

During holidays I work on a farm in Yorkshire. It is too far. I do not like cattle, or mucking out, or getting up early. I visit Rievaulx Abbey. It is broken. This is not what I call entertainment. There is a lot of green.

Appollinaire at the ballet

it grow quick dark redpul-lapart and lights up for greasy
man with loincloth doing the firelighting in a forest
with wavy arms wizard or other homeless like beerbottle
man straw beard he mudstreak no money for clothes do
crouching bendy legs not proper dance then clear off but
nowhere to go then other man young untainted flesh
come on with dead tiger and cod piece and leap about
one leg then other soon fleetfoot out of temple acolyte
maiden run in too of veils she like him lots and do the
leg thing without the sex then another run in tootoo she
smile on him she do the pointy toes like the flower girls
cold outside in stilettos only faster like floating then the
man grab the first lady and toss her up and catch her but
with hand in the bad place she nearly to the fall she duff
him up in the earhole for that in dressing room then he
toss her again and catch her pretty good this time and
he carry her about a bit and she do the wavy arms swan
and longneck like lost in the wrong story then he do
more tossing with the other lady she smile more than
the first lady who look worried the big Russian harps go
thrumski thrumski then all stop for breath and pleased
with that and the audience go mad and throw roses at
the lady but nobody get her because they all crapshot
but she gatherup like nutsinmay only some twigthorns
come off onstage she not bother to gather up then the
first lady do a dance with a basket of red roses she lovely
throw the roses about freehand but there is a snake in
the basket on almighty purpose from the bad other the
man with the codpiece should kill the snake because he
can kill tigers it bite the lady though she carry on for a

bit but sad dying on her pointy legs then not drink the antidote she had enough she lay down the other woman go haha act 2 pull apart reveal the poor clay man fire up hookah for solace to bereaved flesh of all human desire like spice dream opium of the forlorn to vision the dead and the corps de ballet do big entrance with 39 arabesques it go on eternity and look great hurt and the corps de ballet tread on the crapshot thorns so the blood come but they not wince or stopping because they only corps de ballet and need the work after all this is the kingdom of the shades in the interval signormuscelini send a big bouquet of roses to the corps de ballet dressing room he say this time he will have number 4 act 3 redderpart the gods get angry at last and the temple fall apart everybody die but the man and the first lady together in spirit they wake up and it is not a dream and do more slow leaping but they never get to proper lastlong hold in this life the ladies and man come on misery without fulfilment and the painted god down from his pedestal emerging radiant from the dust to take bows the poor man do double act as the god not a full time god just deus ex machina albeit a gilded like born in a barn just remember where he meant to be for one second comebackon he not get much of a look-in hiding in the forest allplay incarnate too late to save the show but all clap anyway for trying only how shall this exonerate shall the play suffice the snake do not come on but bet your nether in the dark root still he lurk all that's left is wraiths in gonewrong story the tossers and the tossed onto the bloodsmear stage with flatfoot dignity celebrants in the triumph of narrative without words after all nowhere to exit but dark all evening in spite of pit deep full of orchestra no-one sings I should have liked one song to sing in the dark even the man with the baton come on and chortle but the corps de ballet do not come on they are only corps de ballet and been on their backs after 39 arabesques and gone home on the bus wraiths without any tea through outcast of thousands counting little purse pennies nursing stigmata past the pointy toe flower girls in the rainy dark on grey pavement in longstanding longing for some moment of dance and light all the lamps pale and yellow but all dragged off behind frayed grey curtain for quick where is not love or money with old sweaty man from taxi with greasy mouth and finger up everywhere and pokey flickery tongue through soundwithoutstoryinfragrantflagrante on soil bed of damp odour of roses in the theatre the audience still shout hooray for 39 arabesques flowergirls and the human condition the next day in the paper the man in the bowtie say the principals do ok in the high drama but the corps de ballet do the cost of living

Theatre functionary

Of course what really got us on our feet was the cleaning contract for Tamburlaine we'd had a huge disappointment with Lear turns out vile jelly only reaches the first two rows well two shots of Cillit Bang and a quick whip round with a mop then there was Titus but there's a limit to what you can do with one solitary tongue a couple of severed hands plus a meagre number of sliced throats the rest of it's a cookery programme pastry just doesn't deliver the same level of shambles Caesar's a dead loss one short scene with concealed daggers and the toga soaks up most of it where's the profit in that as for the Scottish play just a desert of missed opportunities nearly everything happens off stage just a couple more daggers and a load of hand washing yet here's a spot and a little water clears us of this deed I rest my case Hamlet should have delivered with that body count but turned out to be a damp squib plenty of stiffs I grant you but all so sanitised a quick poke through the arras a poisoned goblet and a couple of stage foils no decent hacking just I'll hit him now my lord well don't take all night no for decent consistency of gore give me Tamburlaine every time…

…it's not been easy mind it's a big responsibility delivering a quality finish what with employment rights and finding people who don't mind a bit of blood foreigners of course hardly a word of English and wanting time off for child care as for pension rights don't make me laugh I tell them you're just cleaners not the bloody cast I've had to let no end go with their demands for minimum wage single mothers most of them still at least government's got one thing right getting rid is easy no uncomfortable face to face interviews with tears and pleading or abuse just an anonymous phone call to the authorities a knock on the door in the middle of the night and they're not in the next day and recruitment's dead easy plenty of dinghy rats about as I say we're in clover now Tamburlaine really did it for me there's rivers of blood there's a lot to be said for tyranny.

Déjeuner sur l'herbe.

Such a rare opportunity. After all, everything suited to perfection. A morning of dust, cars overtaking black and tiresome and flowery. Coats dark in such heat. Now at last solid matter of brick pillars against which to compose the will and deposit bicycle. After hard ascent, odour of sweat, misspent urine, mimosa and limes. Cool shade and a bank on which to rest and divest all burden, down to relief of last stitch of tight elastic. *Ecce homo.* The state of nature. Airing one's limbs a great flamboyance. The sole crumb in the ointment fear of bodily creases, the cracks in our humanity, entrapping droppings of crust. The shame of encountering unexpected particles at a critical juncture, with no means of disposal. Having to invent a narrative to a history which is inexplicable, unbearable, jam-ridden. Justice without mercy, the fragile moment collapsing in penile penury.

Unlading of panniers from machine. Carrier bags of tomato, cucumber, meatpaste in glass jars, and apples. Butter half melted but in a sealed container. Nothing shall be lost. Set in the shade to reaffirm. My compact primus and paraffin, two saucers with appropriate cups. Matches. Bone china plates. The half bottle of wine a fortuitous find in a locked cupboard in a dusty vestry. Minimal damage entailed. Digestives also, of identical provenance. Sugar tongs, and milk in a stoppered container. Bread, sliced, a full half loaf, origin impossible to recall but conceivably purloined through the half open casement of a vacant kitchen. Saddlebags equally balanced of water. No need, as it appears. A wall-mounted tap suited to my purposes. And fortuitously a bin for leftovers, though I am disheartened to discover that I am not the first, alone in virgin territory. Other romantics have previously visited, for already it is packed, with husks of dead flowers mainly, dry blooms thrust would not be too strong a word, head first, cellophane wrapped stems protruding from beneath the metal lid. I assay both for perfect function, turning the tap on and off several times, joyfully twisting its little brass handle, and lifting the lid of the bin. Its clangour pleases me. I repeat the operation many times, with increasing volume. To be caught short without means of cleansing unthinkable in such dealings; and to avoid the eviscerating shame of return bearing the half consumed, the undesired. So all in all a great relief. Some dusting necessary; on the ground a former visitor's grey leavings, as if of some style of barbecue or campfire. In my sweeping exertions I inhale their dust. I cough. I cover the patch with a white cloth. Consumption of comestibles and a promised liaison to enhance the day. A perfect location for a first meeting. Such sky. Such airiness. The laying on of cutlery. I consult the diagram on the page removed from *Debretts*, detailing placement of silver. Memory of uncomfortable interview with librarian. Bone handled fish knives for tinned sardines. Cake forks. Tiny dessert spoons for minimalist trifles. Polished to perfection at dawn. Mustard and cruet. I have not neglected the tin opener. Doilies. Crisp napkins, ironed especially for such an eventuality. Small batons of carrot for dipping. For me, dipping is an article of faith. A small baptism. Accoutrements to veniality.

Will it come at last, the dreamed of, longed for theophany. In my quest for suitable private places I reconnoitred many days of long hours and eventually had remarkable luck in my researches. All here is fortunate. Pleasant surroundings, silence, the only buildings far off; gently sloping banks and discrete walls. Regularity their hall mark, discrete plaques, distinct but tasteful print such a pleasure, and an air of municipality. Complemented by an attractive liberality of floral vases. A bloom from each of the freshest to construct a bouquet. This formality suits me well. I relax, free of cares and vestments. An overwhelming tranquility, the only sound the occasional whimper of small dying creatures collapsing through the undergrowth. Today of all days I can be generous, and pity without envy such lives devoid of all hope. The flesh, the grass, the vestiges of a good lunch. What more has life to offer. To meditate upon this bank in a state of innocence, secure in the knowledge that soon it will be done with. With satiety, to lie in the skeletal shade of the conveniently planted rosebush and stroke her hair, adorning her body with occasional petals, imbibing the evanescent odours of love. At nightfall to interrogate the heavens. Until then I have time to spare. I divert myself with the parable of the man and the woodshed. Man owns pile of wood. Has nowhere to store wood. Man uses wood to build shed to store wood. Man has no wood to store in shed. Man demolishes shed. Man left with pile of wood. Enlightenment. Man rebuilds shed. Still no wood to store in shed. Man tears down shed. Left with pile of wood. Nowhere to store pile of wood. Man goes mad because of pile of stinking rotting wood. Decides to hang himself in shed. Man builds shed to hang himself. Pile of wood has miraculously disappeared. Man no longer mad. Then man discovers he is completely devoid of wood to store in shed. Man shrieks and wails, goes mad that he has no wood to store in shed. Tears down shed. Man decides to immolate himself on pile of wood. Wood too wet to burn. Man despairs.

There is infinite solace in the suffering of others.

At last a wheezing and clank of bicycle chain. Sounds of surprised satisfaction at sight of my machine. Discovery. To be found alert and intemperate, at full cock, so to speak, ready and waiting, no preparation lacking. Crunch of footsteps on gravel. A plain suited male figure. Through a portal darkly. This I had not expected. Discussion ensues. An arbiter of propriety. I demur. He has no power, he says, Good, I say. No power he says don't interrupt to evict etc but in terms of public decency, at which point he glances down, at least cover all cooked meats. Threats finally. I explain I have a meeting to attend to. For the sake of common humanity I tell him, I deplore his presence. In the background my small transistor playing quietly. Deaf to all protestations at the need for its muted requiem for purposes of ambience, he insists on silence, attempting to remove its two batteries. I remove two of his teeth. Further blows are exchanged in the spirit of common humanity. Eventually we compromise. I remain but with no saveloy on display. A folded roseate serviette suffices.

Time passed. Exhausted by this encounter, I slept. Waking to a cold sense of abandonment and devastation of half consumed delicacies, among the detritus, pinned beneath the sardine tin, for there was a breeze, I discerned pink paper:

Lovelace.

I cannot believe to what you have brought me; I would not be seen dead in such a place, and after such preparations of bathing, rose water and fresh underwear. In all the fetid sewers of humanity, you are the greatest turd. Your sustenance was a disappointment beyond words, and I, a well brought up young woman from Coggeshall, cannot conceive how you imagined to effect our elopement on an antique bicycle, albeit with two saddles. Neither my morals nor my grammar can be compromised by one of such low standards. I bid you farewell forever, as one whose emotions have been cruelly played upon, or, more correctly, one upon whose emotions have you have cruelly played. Also I recall a prior engagement.

Clara.

PS You will never get your hands on me. My uncle the stockbroker will see to it.

I took this to be a love letter. I cherish it still.

She too had come prepared then; with ink, paper, quill. Means to dry her flowing script. A dictionary and a two volume grammatical manual. A complete escritoire.

Despite all instruction, was this the intended outcome all along, the promised end. In defiance of all instruction, the assertion of her own narrative, throughout the epistolary purgative of our relationship nurturing the gestation of the notional uncle. Her denouement to return to seek the safety of an assumed marriage, leaving one the burden of responsibility to remain the eternal and frequent disappointment, the tragic homunculus in the camera obscura of sexual congress. Full stop.

She had stooped to that last resort of the fugitive exogamist beset by doubt: *avunculus ex machina*. But who shall cast the first stone. Have I not had recourse to a similar device on numerous occasions. I begin to wonder if she herself were not a work of fiction, entirely of her own making.

I meditate upon the grassy bank and the paths of unlost innocence. Evening falls. A glint of moon rising through clouds and a breeze stirring silhouettes of leaves. Soon inevitably a squirrel will pass and an owl hoot. Perhaps the cry of a fox will follow. In the purple distance, white smoke gathering above the tall chimneyed building. The rising fume of humanity. Far off, the endless bleating of lambs. And now ceased, remotely throughout the day, on the fitful breeze, intonation of dirges. Castigations of hope. Was all this not expected. But for these, this day might have been completely lost. Still cause for romance then. Something may be salvaged. I knot all detritus in the blemished cloth and cast it over the wall, a full toss toward the green fomenting pastures, into the unknown, untested regions. There let it rest.

I return home. I enter through the window. As usual, the room is dark. No-one complains.

A perfect match

A real treat for me. He said he would make himself responsible for the meal. He arrived with a pressure cooker. I had done my hair in the special way the women in the office have been advising me, saying it sets off my features. Though not in the first flush of youth, I have worked hard to maintain my figure, and though I say it myself, I am not unattractive.

When the bell rang I hurried down the hallway to greet him and opened the door. I had already removed the safety chain. One does not wish to appear unwelcoming by rattling it and keeping someone waiting when they are expected. I am less concerned with goodbyes.

My aim in life has always been to assist the lonely. It is important to have a purpose. It is almost a passion with me. Everything is prepared.

Internet dating has made things so much easier for me. I would say that my life is almost a joy. I always tried to be thorough in my research: now it is my forte. It is so important if one is to avoid awkward questions. For instance, I know I shall tell the busybodies at work that no-one turned up. I shall shed a few tears. Sympathy is always helpful in these cases. That and cleanliness, especially in the bathroom.

At first sight he seemed a little older than in his photograph. In fact, I found difficulty in recognising him at all. But the outside light is, after all, not functioning, and has not been for some time. Also, as the house looks out onto extremely dark woods, my eyes took a little time to adjust, though I do not suffer from poor eyesight. I can easily read all the labels on the bottles in the medicine cupboard. And of course the woods are familiar to me.

He was standing to one side, a little breathless, looking around and at the upper windows. Even in the poor light, I could see he had had a small accident in his trousers. One should not judge character on such things alone. One cannot have everything. Perhaps he was nervous. Some people are very shy on the first meeting. I invited him in and hung up his thick waterproof. I must confess, it smelt rather strongly. Also his rucksack. He seemed a little dirty, having the air of someone who had come straight from his allotment, from some heavy work like digging, and not taking a proper shower. Still, one cannot have everything. He was wearing a vest under his white shirt. I am not at all keen on this. It seems a dirty habit if not changed every day. My father always wore one, and towards the end it became very unpleasant. It became incumbent upon me to take some action.

He brought a carrier bag of vegetables. Carrots mainly. He said plain was best. It seemed a very large amount for just the two of us. But people like to impress with generosity. He also had a small spatula. Dicing is something in which he delights, he tells me. He says he likes my perfume. Now he is frying onions. My special homemade wine is chilling in the fridge. I have been told its cumulative effect is quite overpowering.

He seems a homely sort of person, enquiring about the neighbours. I take this as a good sign. They are elderly and keep themselves to themselves. He seems satisfied. He has a pleasant smile, though his teeth are a little discoloured. One cannot have everything. He seems a little confused, and keeps trying to lay for six or seven, as though expecting other guests, and looking towards the door. though the table in this flat is very small. Clearly at the end it will be a mercy. I have to be quite firm, reminding him there are just two of us. In other ways he is very organised, keeping a regular check on the time as he prepares. He tells me that at eight fifteen precisely everything will be perfect. He shows me a fine set of knives. I continue to try to make polite conversation but he seems a little withdrawn.

I am still uncertain as to how far I wish to develop this relationship.

I cannot find my phone.

An old retainer

So we enter the great hall, and its magnificent portraits. As in the master bedroom, Venus on the ceiling. Do please feel free to lie on your back for the full experience. On the family shield the legend of the Wormley-Bottomleys—*Digitus in Recto*, that is to say, if my schoolboy Latin has not deserted me, Dignity in all things.

Note the armorial escutcheons granted by royal decree, the crossed cake fork and bloater tongs in recognition of the seventh earl's role in establishing a code of dining etiquette on court occasions, his impeccable manners immortalised in the family motto *Après vous;* a sentiment that has seen the family successfully through numerous generations, adopted in the standing orders for all military engagements from Waterloo to the Somme.

Now we come to The Rochester wing. Inspired by the earl's admiration for Charlotte Bronte's hero of that name in her famous romantic novel, we ask for respectful silence. This is the present Lady Wormley-Bottomley, whom he married to obtain her fortune. The earl's present mistress would have starved her long ago but was persuaded to keep her as a tourist attraction. With considerable success as our numbers today bear witness.

Note the silver hairbrush engraved on the day of their marriage with a touching message, Forever Mine Alone. On her more passive days she is allowed a view of the grounds through the small window, also sight of the pictures of her children as reward for acquiescence. You are politely requested not to take photographs or exhibit signs of sympathy or concern, as likely to encourage false hope. Could she move or speak she would no doubt complain of treachery and abuse, but there are two sides to every story. Indiscretions with the under butler were in violation of the family's strict code of honour, and every established dynasty has it secrets.

This is the end of the tour. You have I hope got what you came for: an insight into how the other, I think I may say better, half conducts itself, a remote sense of pity, and a note of melodrama. Tea rooms and toilets are located down the stairs. The chocolate orange drizzle cake is especially recommended. Here is the balustrade I mentioned earlier, over which the third earl pushed his second wife. A thousand piece jigsaw of the tapestry celebrating this event is available for purchase. Souvenir tea towels are for sale in the gift shop, as are colouring books for the children, recounting the story of the earl's present wife and mistresses. Also there are books on the history of economics of the slave trade, with colour illustrations. These are now located in the Business and Self Help section.

Thank you. That's most kind. We are all volunteers and do it because we love it. Yes, such an ancient family. The stories do bring it to life. No direct connection, no, though there was a time... The broken promise and the poor girl in the Deer Pond? Thank you, sir. A long time ago but everything to us. I do my best to keep my spirits up, though there are of course many days... Narrative is so important. We can only obey its imperative. Other guides may give a completely different impression, but I always like to take tourists through the private quarters when the earl is absent. Mind the stairs. After you.

'Et in Arcadia Ego': A Man of Letters.

Again, in fulfilment of my promise, I stand beside you. Today I bring roses. Their scent, your breath. Trust me, they shall not wither. They shall be removed, every last petal, even before the radiance begins to depart. Before the vulgar hint of mortality, the slab swept clean. There shall be no dishonour to love.

ISA BEL L A, do you remember so long ago now, how once we talked of the King of Spain's daughter, in the grove among the linnets? All piping song and rustling among the leaves. Of how all begins and ends in love, the pinnacle and perfection of all feeling? That it teaches much of pain, imposing the harsh necessity of our beguilings, forming imaginings more real than mere distance, or this cruel division of centuries? What purpose art but to frame our passion; to eschew all platitudes, and rise above the clichés of existence? Once again I calculate your years, eighteen, so few: the very reason, from among so many, you alone I chose to be my own. So much that might have been.

So many have tried to forbid me this place; insisting it is wrong to appropriate the grief of others; telling me this must end, a mere fiction, a fantasy, a chimera, not understanding how you haunt these stones, you, my own creation. That confers certain rights. Without me you are nothing; mere dust and corrupted soil, your only adornments damp splinters of elm. Without me you remain forgotten, your life empty, your death meaningless. I am the resurrection, my word the retraction of the worm. I alone to breathe life into your words, my fingers alone to caress your small breasts, know the secrets of your body.

And the gifts of an unlived life I bring you. Our whole family together at rest. The little ones. Such memories of our own precious unborn. The days spent in hide and seek. A warm spring of primroses. The picnic by the lake. What you whispered to me that day. Our losses. They say I should not torment myself. But to be parted from you. When I hear a child lisping rhymes, or the song of the linnet, who would not choose such? What the alternative? Remembering how the nights flew as we danced, the stars reeling, the dream of crossing seas together, staring out from the bow on the white foam, your skin pale in the moonlight—the Grand Tour: Venice, Florence. Through the galleries of perfect forms. To me you are nothing less. And the triumphant return; in my arms at the threshold. In the orchard, fruits ripening to gold.

And the days that followed. That summer dress, your hair. Bright ribbons. Waiting in dappled shade. Gathering nuts. Your laughter as you ran through leaves, the twisting path narrowing, until you turned, breathless, to face me, the linnets singing, my hands upon your waist. Unloosing the ribbons, your hair falling, your breath coming faster. Afterwards, how you sang of the little tree that bore only magical fruit. The day I first imagined the pallor on your cheek. The lonely privilege of the literary mind to grow so enamoured with tragedy. Figurings more real than snows or this shower. This bench. Such irony, such cruelty in the impermanence of stone but the relentless integrity of feeling. How I treasure that memory of Florence, before those images of the eternal Virgin. I could have knelt and worshipped you then, before the crowds, weeping at the beauty of it all.

Then the nights at the embassy! *The Spanish Ambassador.*

'In the late spring of—, as the war with P— was reaching its crisis, the city was garrisoned by the —th Regiment of the King's Hussars. At that time it was the custom for the Ambassador to host...'

The glittering chandeliers. The silver. At dinners, the Spanish ambassador's head bent close to you in conversation. Then gifts. Flowers at first. Later, jewels. To lay upon your breast.

That night, making towards the carriages, down the long mirrored corridor, the rustle of your silk dress, suddenly his swarthy hand upon you. How I struck him then. The shrieks of women. Angry shouts of men. The challenge. To hear him say that I—I!—was delusional! The newspapers all on my side. The interview with the Prime Minister. At last, the courtroom hushed, and my vindication. A complete victory. His dismissal. The riotous applause. On the balcony, crowds cheering. Waving, hearing the accolades. Would it ever hold together, could I ever convince with such a tale? Paragraphs, chapters, reworked. Reimaginings. Your indiscretion then , no, your infidelity, no—Never believe it of you. None would believe it. None could countenance such an end to our romance.

A whole volume wasted then. Into the fire.

So now this. Though I have longed for your touch through the weary change of so many seasons, tracing out the letters of a name now worn with love's attrition, I grow resigned to the knowledge this could never be. Never have been. Casting the nights for pain, probing the depths of the wound, the implacable slow erosions of love. A world of fierce temptations, the pain of impossibilities. The beginning, and soon an end; let it be in this place, among these green boughs, hearing this song. It is enough.

You do not speak now as once you did. Silences grow longer; my vision of you less clear.

Light falls differently. The pettiness of these clouds! The dreary, futile transience of nature!

The city wakes. Traffic and crowds quicken through the streets. Pressing their narratives from Southwark, Walworth, Newington, the legendary lands of the sweet Infanta, they move for the sake of the pure envisioned.

In the silver case, the gold ring, and this, in the place known only to ourselves.

As always, I leave my glove for you to know I will come again.

Michelangelo among the fishcakes

A gladsome day. A morning of mistaken trams and caustic remarks. Apollinaire and Cassandra with limited resources and intentions of the grand tour, address the coiling worm for the Ufizzi, wilting half around the block. Her prophetic observation re the likelihood of ingress within the next millennium accepted without surprise: a truth taken like medicine to be an exaggeration born of sunstroke. Frequent examination of her wristwatch added point. Dangling loose, a sartorial crime, evidence of another failure of his judgement, this falling in the time of gifts of the Nativity. A burden and irritation to its owner, its bracelet overgenerous on a slender wrist, a cause of relentless fist shaking, with the sound of a mobile ossuary. Other crimes to be taken into account and held against him: hotel booking, cancelled by mop bearing proprietor on arrival—Not my fault, the pointless excuse; failures in the plumbing—Consequent hunt in faltering Italian through dimly lit streets for clean sheets and breakfast at reasonable budget. Failed attempts at humour—No en suite, my sweet.

After an hour lobstered under the sun the *homo erectus* of replica David hove into view. This enticing spectacle of hope and encouragement dashed by a fast moving second queue of pre-bookers strolling through the shaded portals. This she observed, but said nothing. Salt in a considerable wound. A whole lamentable cruet. Abandon all hope, ye without papers. Here they stuck for twenty minutes, she eyeing the toned torso readied to face its Goliath; he unable to determine whether her interest lay in toned physicality or its murderous intent.

At the arrival of several bodies of nuns all with the necessary, she offered a tearful valediction along the lines of she would be violated in the anal region if forced to abide longer, and would be departing this mortal coil in quest of sustenance, her internal arrangements having been distorted beyond endurance and possibly beyond repair by lack of comestibles and foresight. Woe unto him, the sandwiches freshly cut that morning, layered with adjuncts of humus and mayonnaise, lay forgotten on the island, an accusation awaiting his return, like a dog unto. Technically then the sight was over— not fore—But who would dare to question her at this juncture? He gathered up her rucksack as she made off through the legions, seeking what would have been, had they washed up in another city, a Rubicon.

In the clarity of his despair he noted her shadow perfectly aligned with the parting form, and the zenith past, with no other course of action available, determined to follow the trajectory of Earth's dying star. Through the pizza oven of an afternoon in search, a faithful Dobbin, bearer of many burdens, including guilt of man's inadequacy to woman, closeted within her pink rucksack, Item: one sweater, cashmere, rose, fleece of the horned one, item one mobile telephone, Samsung, on contract, one purse wallet style containing cards of multiple credit, one permit to drive motorised vehicles for private and domestic use, item one passport, containing inadequate photographic resemblance of the beloved, item twenty euros cash. Item one bottle nail varnish with brush attachment, blushing pink, selected through mysteries of the craft to adorn and complement the hue of aforementioned cashmere sweater. Item, one bottle perfume, aerosol nozzle, eau de Gare du Nord. Miscellaneous items, one hairbrush, one mirror, makeup, shades various, one publication entitled *Top Ten things to do in*, containing Explorers' map, In profound secretive pockets: Item, matters various relating to the female anatomy, item one pair of spare undergarments, lace, black. Should he fail in this quest, her position up this particular creek of the Arno would find her well and truly paddleless.

Eventually after a tour of thoroughfare and backstreet, discovered eating fishcakes outside a small crowded restaurant. His tentative approach in hope the return of precious cargo, viz. her phone and purse, might act as peace offering, going off much as the welcome of Captain Cooke in Hawaii. She had joined a table of young men and women, students he supposed, all laughing. When they caught sight of him, bepinked with rucksack, and mirth abruptly ceased, it was clear whither their bolts were targeted. He could gauge her relief and delight on seeing him by the manner in which she hailed him as a Penelope on the return of Ulysses, with characteristic smile and friendly inquiry as to where in the name of sexual congress he had absented himself hitherto.

Nonetheless, accommodation was offered, by a greeting with only a hint of accent and sarcasm. The knife twisted as he perceived the keen flash of her eyes and realised this *vivace* he had not seen in weeks; also, alas, the proximity of her muscular neighbour, leaning in and fingering her bare forearm every time she spoke, and even presuming to adjust the loose watchstrap on her wrist, inserting his finger within its circlet. He marvelled at her ability to contort her figure, with a skill beyond yoga, so as to address the assembled company whilst constantly rotating her back in his direction. He thought of the other miracle, of the divinely composed and wholly unlikely arm of David, poised with its slingshot. Here was a chip off the old.

One of the young men, dark bespectacled, began to commiserate at the day's revelations of the vanity of all desire: the disarray of timetables and the young lady's hair, so becoming, mere indications of their failed excursion to visit our David... That it fell within the remit of this particular beast viz the visual arts, to decry the vanity of all human disposition; what after all was an afternoon between the covers of wasted passion, in comparison to a Van Rijn, or that marvel in marble, or the beauty of an unacknowledged desire for contract with the florist, or an unrequited passion for the woman next door whose washing line had become his daily study; and here the intrusive digit brought closer its maw redolent of garlic, 'For a woman who is not serious about her underwear cannot be trusted with one's emotions.' Apollinaire adjusted his seat.

He offered a non—committal response. Undeterred the speculum continued, that no explanation were needed—yes, he even resorted to the frailty of the subjunctive, such is the finesse of English teaching in modern foreign language schools: *In conclusion merely, it is an oft noted effect.*

Not understanding, he apologised, not feeling the need to apologise, or to understand. He still held her purse and phone. These were powerful cards.

The diatribe continued on the topic of the advantages of disappointment, and the power and beauty of acceptance. *The exquisite torment of life... So fruitful...*

He endured the dialectic of *ars longa* with the grace of a *memento mori*.

Their outcry: they sing without voices a hymn to our inadequate response to beauty. They endure without passion, violating all our discourse, the perfected sexless forms excoriating our precepts and every effort to sustain the thought of mere mortality...

He could not but applaud the language while lamenting the sentiment. But he had discovered other fish to fry. He had designs upon a plate of discarded linguini. For had he not, like a proper Christian, fasted since yesterday? He had assiduously kept flies from this votive offering, and throughout the lecture had busied himself beneath the folds of the tovaglia in engineering an implement, let us with humanity call it a spoon, from the remains of a cigarette packet. Let it not be said that a little in the way of ash and dogends would deter the certain poor from myrrh, among other gifts of frankincense and wisdom from such as these.

As he made ready for a secretive foray into these comestibles he was thwarted by the approach of the waistcoat and pad who swept all before him. Only a caraf of water remained. He took this to be symbolic:

there would be no wedding at Cana today. He thought of the tiny jewel box carried close to his breast, and examined the vacuity of blue air interlacing the rooftops. Should we then be silent?

Meanwhile in the profound and fetid darks of the back kitchen, the restaurant manager quizzed the chef, a temporary replacement from the small Sicilian village of Sotto Passagio. His curiosity had been piqued at the sight of a patty of fish particles and potato, lurking on the plate of a female customer, not available on the menu, like Moncrieff's cucumber, not even for ready money. Under interrogation, the chef pointed to a lesser visited corner of the kitchen and cried that he saw the fishcake in the freezer, and carved until he set it free.

As the sun dipped over the Arno, it fell to our protagonist to pay everyone's bill. Such is the fount of generosity of the arts. At last, having been warned in a vision of further designs upon their wallets, our lovers hotwired a Vespa and returned by another way.

It was at this point, heads bent over corroded terminals, that a discussion had ensued, which may in some small way have contributed to the beginnings of salvation. For how then should they proceed; he without knowledge of the labyrinthine streets, she in a skirt short and unduly tight? In the words of the ethereal messenger, Fear not; for the Italian spirit, though passionate, has refinement, and years of experience have led to solutions both practical and aesthetic in the negotiation of traffic; and the seat of a Vespa being neither the time nor occasion for the conjunction of intellects or genitalia, Reader, she rode an elegant sidesaddle *alla moda Italiana,* as she had many times observed with admiration; and, with modesty preserved, navigating from the pillion by moonlight and street lamp from the folds of the creased map burrowed from her rucksack, directing by a form of communication contrived for the circumstance—that is to say, by elbow: one bruise in the ribs for left, two for right, a flurry of blows for a wrong turn, as on il terzo giro of the magic gloom of the Duomo, In the space of ten minutes, bareheaded they pass Christ crowning the Virgin three times in stained glass above the liturgical clock, with a pitiful cry from the postillion, that one divine coronation should be enough. And comes the desolate complaint to windward of so much cartography, so little light; for secretly long before she had shed all faith in printed matter and trusted to stellar navigation. Thus they proceeded in their inglorious transit. And when fuel and big end finally expired, they abandoned the spent wasp at the shuttered door of a convent, that the sisters might discover it and, mindful of Macarius' donkey, pray for their sins to be forgiven them. And from here they walked, guided by starlight and the aroma of pizza, arriving at an upper room with aching feet and hearts, he bearing the rucksack and part of the weight of her upper body, a pieta. It is finished.

Much later, deep into a long night, and only after the manager had respectfully tapped the door repeatedly with both fists to enquire whether the shouting would be continuing, and if so, how the stones of the street would better suit as domicile; there were other guests who knew better how to behave and enjoy their visit to the heart of culture, did they after muchel care and wo come to terms and settle their differences with—believe it who may—a liaison of violent tenderness, with shutters wide to a sky of stars, and a breeze from the Arno caressing the moonlit rooftops. Somewhere someone is singing, as they must, given the romantic circumstances, *Salce Salce* from Otello.

Inside the darkened Ufizzi, the true David stood, constant, dynamic, silent and alone; with a handful of nothing but stones to sustain him in his endeavour, and thus a parable for life, yet ready to conquer; immaculate and towering, confident and solitary on his plinth. An impossibility carved from a flawed block, someone else's failure. In much vaunted phrase, someone had eyed up the angel in the marble. So far, so good, but a serious amount of chisel work lay ahead. And in the Duomo the unresolved dual perspectives of the condottieri remain to trouble us.

From galleries of busts, to bust ups, to the adoration of the upper reaches of the beloved torso—for alas, in our travails, we have stooped this high—who can escape the vagaries and resonance of language? And though what guides the chisel is passion and skill, starting from the right or even the wrong block counts for something. And if destiny is discovered intent upon the consumption of fishcakes in dubious company, who can deny fate? The concurrences of art and language may save them yet: from life's imperative they extracted a narrative and achieved the wisdom of silence. Though they never stood in contemplation at the feet of David, life granted compensations: a view of the Arno from a tall storey, a song in the dark, and a post coital repast of sandwiches only slightly curled.

What more then of our protagonists, sleeping off a long delayed, long endured passion? After all, had she not, in the most private folds of her rucksack, prophesied how it must be? Shouting and kissing are mutually exclusive: having failed in one might they not with justice attempt the other? Explanations, none satisfactory, mutual weepings on forgiving shoulders, and the due consideration of formulae concerning potential gains against effort required, were long discussed, and set aside unproven, with the sad finale that though it be highly desirable to travel a while among the Old Masters, it is impossible to endure that degree of perfection in such large volumes. It's too overwhelming. Surely, holding that pose, even a David's arm must ache. To say nothing of his heart. Sometimes you just need plain fare.

Which is what they purchased the next morning, and a small box having been produced at an appropriate time with due ceremony, returned to almost satisfactory existences of near respectability, with hardly more than the usual level of disappointment, and consoled themselves occasionally with comfortably remote dreams of the rebirth of learning.

And if punning be the lowest form of wit, and the subjunctive the true habitation of our desires, say on. Not all art is great, nor all greatness artful. Let us still stand respectfully before the angelic marble and its victory over dual perspectives, body and soul, with the only suitable response, for this too may prove an egregious dichotomy.

Or in other words

Tacet.

And so to bed

the stairs by candlelight arraign the day ghosts wreath
these walls I write them full moon the dark dreams the
dark set aside the flame into the shadowlands make light
of dream the ebb of feeling clasp of hands that dance
with a girl green-eyed and hair flowing on the music
birds soar on a silk gown a door kicked in brother's boots
at the frame locked out the exiles so much blood so
much dancing where did that phone go never resolved
that one that poor fellow gave him half a crown hardly
recompense for his daughter how the other half single
glove on a slab never get to sleep after that lot

no more sundays all dead now the choir master blue
rinse ladies of the parish tyranny over cake and
sandwich why walk away their constant interrogation
who do you think you all staring darkness creeping the
church empty dusty pews now all silent and the street
empty revellers all departed not a song to sing set aside
this candlelight all those arabesques shadow now

birds ripple on her curves shadow of the Duomo tiny
points of light gone midnight suppressed laughter
outside the shuttered convent settling our differences
books half written rewritten abandoned the dead girl's
stone when will it all end candlelight the game worth is
it

to prayers then window ajar so in the morning scent of
fresh bread an epiphany Lord shall these things never be
again no-one listening not even me gave up long ago
knees too old to bend mind atrophied Lord give us a

break I may wake to birdsong not to live by it alone

there should be a fire in this room make cheese on toast London in flames the great observer digging a hole for his priorities

at the children's party I alone seated dreaming then wake frozen with fear all standing for prayers me unable to move all accusing we can't start why don't you Christ knows Amen

thought I was taking the what I'm doing now down the sink I can't be bothered just let me be run the cold sluice it away no evidence expect it all goes into the same sewer we all do

bollocking from the rector afterwards christian rectitudes pouring out of his rectum I was four   fuck the lot of them can't you just leave me in peace seventy years and you can't forget a thing like that

you'll never get all this down shot of it all no time for madeleines second time I've used that joke is it a joke I thought I was serious I was once before all this trouble well out of the frying pan into the covers for sweet oblivion Lord let it be soon

is the day then done with me let them haunt me still I think of the dancing the little Irish maid and the bra-less Cossack firm-titted was ever such music don't start not the time or how many nights left shots in the dark I should do something write something maybe get up to something light a candle maybe the muse will come to amuse me *amuse bouche* 69 that's filthy what does it matter all this is bollocks it's all been bollocks every damn thing all about bollocks it starts in someone else's bollocks and ends in our own

different for women of course it doesn't work with eggs

why bother with all this just sleep it off the cattle and sheep in the fields out all night birds roosting what do they know happy in instinct alone it all may come to something time to reflect all those painters why so many self-portraits look at Rembrandt look at me and again this need to know who we are making images it's not what's in the mirror it's the mind they're painting I blame no-one not even God what would be the point those futile atheists you've got to find something not to believe in end in a preposition let it pass I'm half cut half asleep those humble little words working hard to place us in time and space small things have great power a lady at a bus stop giving away biscuits almost forced to believe in human nature any more than I asked her to darn my socks and I'd no idea what she meant when she said Northern Soul do northerners have different souls maybe it's the mountains or is it moors catholics better souls than protestants and where does that leave the non-conformists still wanting to marry their dead wife's sister

turn again Whittington try this side that damned cat yowling again after all the females good luck with that all dark now moon gone down stars dying given billions of years all will be dark cold meaning expired can't wait that long it's all temporary sic transit but there were moments chasing up the stairs laughing I should have

made a better job of all this not so much to wonder at in
the night or dread the dusk the dark so long the page
blank the fear
how could they not
flee from these cruel arms
to kinder embrace

not enough in that confession alone not poetry they'd
just had enough Coleridge even in his lime tree bower
setting off a whole genre of conversational making it
look easy damn him but thwarted all his suppressed
anxieties never finishing with his man from Porlock but
confession came after all that ancient mariner horrors
welling up from the depths searching for benison a
twisted leg the least of his worries

I may wake to the smell of new bread a risen hope why
do we say night falls when really we turn away from the
light moon down all the lights extinguished and stars
dying that is their brightness dreaming our essence I
asked my friend in high pretentiousness I was young is
there art in life he put me straight no just ways of getting
by dreaming now the dark dreaming the dark its own
portrait it's all chance still better luck than never eyes
down then a song a dance there was a ship why so grim
anon anon sir aslant into eternity

www.ingramcontent.com/pod-product-compliance
Lightning Source LLC
Chambersburg PA
CBHW021346060726
47591CB00006B/2179